This book belongs to

....

This edition published by Parragon Books Ltd in 2016

Parragon Books Ltd
Chartist House
15–17 Trim Street
Bath BA1 1HA, UK
www.parragon.com

ISBN 978-1-4748-5288-3

Printed in China

DISNEY
M🌺ANA

Book of Destiny

PaRRagon

Bath · New York · Cologne · Melbourne · Delhi
Hong Kong · Shenzhen · Singapore

Moana was a little girl who lived with her family on the island of Motunui. Her home was a beautiful place, surrounded by a coral reef and shimmering blue seas.

Her father, Tui, was the chief of the island. Moana was destined to be chief too, one day.

Chief Tui cared very much about his people and made sure they were happy and safe. He didn't allow anyone to sail beyond the coral reef, where it might be dangerous.

After all, Motunui had everything the villagers needed. Who would ever want to leave?

One day, Moana's Gramma Tala
was telling a story to the children in
the village.

"Long ago, there was an island
goddess called Te Fiti," she began.
"All life sprang from her heart.
But one day, the giant demigod
Maui took her heart. As Maui
made off, a fire demon called Te Kā
attacked him and the heart was lost
to the sea forever."

The children were terrified –
all except little Moana, who loved
her grandma's stories.

Later that day, Moana was playing by the sea when the seawater magically rose up around her. She saw a spiral stone in the water and grasped it.

Just then, Chief Tui came looking for his daughter. As he picked up Moana, she dropped the stone.

Gramma Tala had been secretly watching from the bushes. She picked up the spiral stone before a wave washed it away.

Time passed. When Moana was 16 years old, Chief Tui
took her to climb the island's highest mountain.

"One day, you will add your stone to this mountain,"
he said, "and raise our whole island higher."

Tui told Moana how important it was for her to stay in the village and lead her people. Moana wanted to make her father proud, but she couldn't help wondering what might be out there, beyond the coral reef.

Later that day, Gramma Tala took Moana to a
secret cave. Moana couldn't believe her eyes – the
cave was filled with sailing boats! The boats belonged
to their ancestors, who had been voyagers.

Gramma Tala explained that after Maui stole Te Fiti's heart, darkness took over the seas. The ancient chiefs stopped Moana's people from sailing to keep them safe.

"The darkness will spread to our island too, unless someone finds Maui and takes him to restore Te Fiti's heart," said Gramma Tala, "and the sea chose you." She gave the spiral stone to Moana. It was actually the heart of Te Fiti!

Soon after, Gramma Tala passed away. With her last
breath, she told Moana to find Maui.

Moana took a little boat from the cave and set sail.
But soon, a storm rose up. A giant wave crashed into her
boat and everything faded to black.

When Moana woke up, she was on a strange beach.

Suddenly, Maui appeared. Moana had landed on his island!

Moana asked Maui to help her restore Te Fiti's heart, but he refused – he wanted to find his magical fishhook instead. The hook gave him the power to shape-shift into different animals, and he'd lost it in his battle with Te Kā. Maui trapped Moana in a cave and took her boat to go and search for his hook.

Moana was determined not to let Maui get away. She escaped from the cave and dived into the sea just as Maui set sail.

Suddenly, the sea pulled Moana under the water and placed her on the boat!

"You will put back the heart!" Moana said in her bravest voice, holding the spiral stone out to him.

But Maui still refused to help her.

As Moana and Maui argued, spears started landing around them. They were being attacked by the Kakamora – little coconut-clad bandits.

Both Maui and Moana fought back against the tiny pirates until they were able to sail away.

Maui was impressed by Moana's bravery. He finally agreed to go with her to find Te Fiti, but said they would never succeed without his shape-shifting powers. They needed to find his fishhook first.

Maui was pretty sure who had his hook – Tamatoa, a giant crab who loved to collect treasures. Tamatoa lived in Lalotai, the realm of the monsters. By the next morning, Moana and Maui had reached the tall, rocky island that was the entrance to the realm.

The friends climbed up the steep rock and finally reached the peak. Moana and Maui each took a deep breath and jumped into the pitch-black hole that led into Lalotai.

In another world under the ocean, Moana and Maui found themselves in a huge, dark cavern.

Suddenly, Moana saw the hook, hidden in a pile of treasures. But just then, the ground rose up to reveal Tamatoa, who pinned Maui to the ground.

Thinking quickly, Moana held out the stone from her necklace.

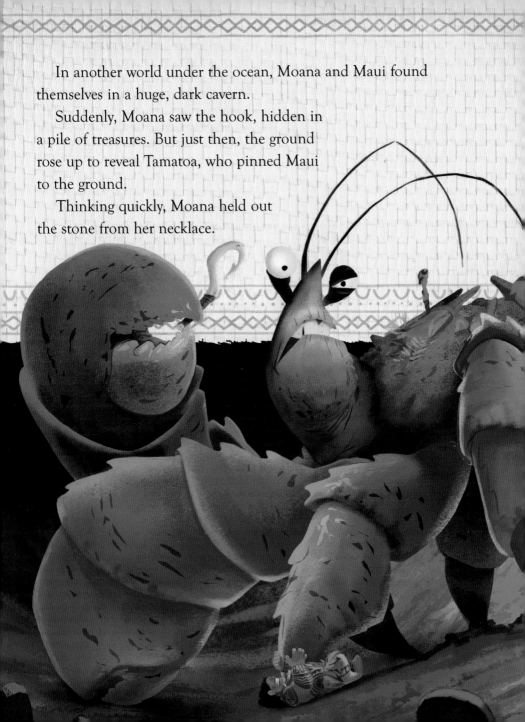

Tamatoa scrambled to snatch the stone – he couldn't resist new treasures. Moana grabbed the hook, but then dropped the stone as she and Maui escaped.

"But – the heart!" cried Maui.

"He can have it, I've got this one," Moana whispered, as she opened her hand to reveal the real heart of Te Fiti. Moana had tricked Tamatoa with an ordinary rock!

Before the monster could attack, a geyser exploded underneath the two friends, launching them out through the top of the realm.

The pair travelled onwards to find Te Fiti. They were nearly there! But as they approached the island, Te Kā suddenly appeared out of a cloud of ash. Maui transformed himself into a hawk using his hook, but Te Kā knocked Maui from the sky.

Moana caught Maui in her boat and headed back towards Te Fiti. Maui tried to stop her: "We won't make it! Moana, turn back."

Te Kā's fist slammed downwards to crush their boat, but at the last second, Maui changed himself back into his human form and raised his hook to block Te Kā's fist.

A huge wave swept Moana, Maui and the boat far away. Moana wanted to go back, but Maui refused. Te Kā's blow had cracked the demigod's precious hook. Maui turned into a hawk again and angrily flew off.

Moana spoke to the sea with tears in her eyes. "I couldn't make it. You'll have to choose someone else," she said, heartbroken. Then she held the heart out to the sea and a wave reached up and took it back.

Just then, the spirit of Gramma Tala appeared and said that she would always be with Moana, whatever she decided to do.

Suddenly, hundreds of ghostly canoes emerged from the sea, and a chorus of voices rose up. "Know who you are," the voices chanted. They were the spirits of Moana's voyaging ancestors.

Moana realized that she would be the one to restore Te Fiti's heart. She dived over the side of her boat and took the heart back from the sea bed.

Back on her boat, Moana headed towards Te Fiti once again.
Te Kā wanted to stop her. But just before Te Kā struck Moana,
Maui appeared out of nowhere to take the blow!

While Maui and Te Kā battled on, Moana reached Te Fiti.
But something was terribly wrong: the island was just an empty
crater, and the goddess was nowhere to be seen.

Te Kā swooped down in front of Moana, but the demon no longer seemed frightening. Trusting her instincts, Moana reached out and placed the heart into Te Kā's chest. She watched as the face of the lava monster transformed. Now that the goddess's heart was restored, she was changing back to her true self.

Te Fiti opened her hand to reveal Maui's hook, fixed – she had forgiven him. Te Fiti's island exploded with flowers and came back to life, at last.

Back on Motunui, Tui was very worried about his
missing daughter. But then Moana appeared on the
horizon, and Chief Tui and the villagers of Motunui
were overjoyed.

Moana had restored Te Fiti's heart, which meant her people could sail safely across the sea again, just as they had done long ago.

Moana finally knew who she was – the next great explorer, destined to lead her tribe on amazing new adventures.

Meet Moana

Moana lives on a beautiful island called Motunui with her family.

Moana loves the sea and wants to explore it more than anything in the world!

She is destined to be the chief of her island one day, just like her father. She really wants to make him proud.

MOANA'S FACT FILE

Age: 16

Best friend: Pua the pig

Most prized possession: Gramma Tala's necklace

Top skill: wayfinding

Moana's favourite thing about herself is ... that she is brave.

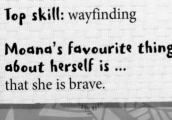

Meet Maui

Maui is a mischievious demigod who loves to trick people and always tries to get his own way.

He is able to shape-shift to take the form of any animal, but he can't do it without the help of his magical fishhook!

MAUI'S FACT FILE

Age: unknown

Favourite place: the open sea

Most prized possession: his magical fishhook

Top skill: shape-shifting

Maui's favourite thing about himself is ... that he is a 'hero of men'!

Many years ago, Maui stole the heart of Te Fiti, so Moana has hunted him down to make him put it back.

All about you

Stick in a photo or draw a picture of yourself here.

Name: ....

Age: ....

Birthday: ....

Hair colour: ....

Eye colour: ....

My best friend's name is: ....

My most prized possession is: ....

My favourite place is: ....

....

Something that makes me special is: ....

....

Something that I love doing is: ....

....

....

Family Fun

Moana lives with her her dad Chief Tui, her mum Sina and her funny Gramma Tala. She loves them all very much and wants to make them proud. Write all about your own family here.

Who is the eldest? ....

Who is the youngest? ....

Do you have any pets? ....

Who gives the best hugs? ....

Who is the bravest? ....

Who tells the best jokes? ....

How would your family describe you? ....

....

....

Circle the words that best describe your family!

Talented   Noisy   Big   Fun
Small   Silly   Calm   Happy

Stick in a photo or draw a picture of your family here.
Don't forget to write down who's who!

Personal paradise

Motunui is a beautiful island paradise with lots of coconut trees and sunshine. What would YOUR personal paradise look like? It could be anywhere in the world, so let your imagination run wild!

Draw your paradise below!

Give your paradise a name:

....

Who would live there with you?

....

My paradise would be:

- ◯ A tropical island
- ◯ A big city
- ◯ A quiet village
- ◯ A jungle
- ◯ A desert
- ◯ Another planet

My paradise would have:

- ◯ A cinema
- ◯ Restaurants and cafés
- ◯ Sandy beaches
- ◯ Flower-filled meadows
- ◯ A shopping centre
- ◯ A sparkling river

In my paradise, it would always be ...

- ◯ Sunny
- ◯ Snowing
- ◯ Raining

Describe a perfect day in your paradise:

....

....

....

Explore the world

Moana has wanted to explore the sea ever since she was a little girl. What kind of adventurer would you be? Use the key below to figure out what your unique explorer name is!

First letter of your first name:

A = Valiant
B = Brave
C = Expert
D = Fantastic
E = Confident
F = Strong
G = Great
H = Courageous
I = Bold
J = Fearless
K = Lionhearted
L = Heroic
M = Talented
N = Brilliant
O = Famous
P = Master
Q = Outstanding
R = Extraordinary
S = Skilful
T = Terrific
U = Spectacular
V = Magnificent
W = Impressive
X = Excellent
Y = Gifted
Z = Amazing

First letter of your second name:

A = Adventurer
B = Wanderer
C = Voyager
D = Wayfinder
E = Seeker
F = Climber
G = Explorer
H = Discoverer
I = Sailor
J = Hunter
K = Traveller
L = Mountaineer
M = Navigator
N = Diver
O = Pioneer
P = Searcher
Q = Venturer
R = Investigator
S = Tracker
T = Sea Captain
U = Journeyer
V = Mountaineer
W = Wayfarer
X = Pilot
Y = Finder
Z = Aviator

I AM

....
(write your own first name here)

THE

.... **!**
(1st explorer word)   (2nd explorer word)

What places would you like to explore?

1. ....

2. ....

3. ....

4. ....

List any special exploring equipment you might need to bring with you:

1. ....

2. ....

3. ....

4. ....

Draw a picture of yourself as an explorer here!

Terrific tattoos

Maui has lots of magical tattoos. Each one represents a special moment in his life. Try designing a cool tattoo for each of your favourite memories. Be imaginative!

Describe your special memory here:

....

....

....

....

....

Draw the tattoo here:

Circle the place where this tattoo would go:

Describe your special memory here: ....
....
....

Circle the place where this tattoo would go:

Draw the tattoo here:

Describe your special memory here: ....
....
....

Circle the place where this tattoo would go:

Draw the tattoo here:

Follow your dreams

Ever since she was a little girl, Moana has dreamed of sailing the sea and exploring the world. Gramma Tala encourages Moana to explore her dreams and be who she is meant to be!

Dream job:
- ○ Writer
- ○ Explorer
- ○ Doctor
- ○ Pilot
- ○ Singer
- ○ Chef

Something else ....

Always remember who you are.

Dream home:
- ○ Castle
- ○ Mansion
- ○ Cottage
- ○ Apartment
- ○ Igloo
- ○ Submarine

Something else ....

Dream pet:
- ○ Pig
- ○ Dog
- ○ Unicorn
- ○ Tiger
- ○ Parrot
- ○ Bunny

Something else ....

Write down your biggest hopes, dreams and wishes here:

....

....

....

....

....

....

....

....

....

....

....

....

....

Discover your destiny

Moana discovers that she is destined to be a great wayfinder and lead her people across the sea. Take this quiz to discover what you are destined to be!

1 **How would you spend your perfect Saturday?**

a. Hiking in the forest
b. Painting or drawing
c. A fun day out with your best friends

2 **What is your favourite kind of sport?**

a. Diving, climbing, trampolining ... something adventurous
b. A brand new sport that you have invented
c. Anything, as long as you get to be team captain!

3 **You and your friends are planning a birthday party. You offer to ...**

a. Find the perfect venue
b. Make the birthday cake
c. Send out the invitations

4 You've just moved to a new school. What's the first thing you do?

a. Sign up for a school trip
b. Check out the science lab
c. Start a new school club

5 How would you describe your sense of style?

a. I'm adventurous
b. I'm unique
c. I'm a trend-setter

MOSTLY As:

An Explorer. You're curious and brave, and love to go on big adventures.

MOSTLY Bs:

An Inventor. You love to create and invent things, and have tons of great ideas.

MOSTLY Cs:

A Leader. People look up to you, and you're great at organizing things.

Ocean adventures

Moana's journey across the sea is super exciting – and a little bit scary. She battles monsters, escapes from pirates and learns to navigate just like her ancestors. Have you ever gone on a big journey? Write about it here.

Where did you go?..

How did you get there?
- ◯ Plane
- ◯ Bus
- ◯ Boat
- ◯ Bike
- ◯ Train
- ◯ Car
- ◯ Helicopter
- ◯ On foot

Who did you go with?

....

How long was the journey?

....

What was the most exciting part?

....

....

How did it make you feel?
- ◯ Excited
- ◯ Happy
- ◯ Homesick
- ◯ Nervous
- ◯ Tired
- ◯ Giddy

Now plan a trip that you would like to take when you are older. It could be to anywhere in the world – or even to another galaxy! Don't forget to include who you would bring with you and how you would get there.

Let your imagination run wild!

....

....

....

....

....

....

....

....

....

....

....

....

Animal antics

Moana loves her animal friends – they may be small, but they have big personalities!

Pua

Pua is Moana's super-cute pet pig. He would do anything for Moana and hates being away from her. Pua loves food, and he sometimes behaves a bit like a puppy!

Heihei

Heihei is a silly rooster who lives in Moana's village. He gets confused a lot. He accidentally goes with Moana on her journey across the sea and causes lots of trouble!

Write about your own animal friends here!

If you don't have any animal pals, make some up. Have fun!

Name:

....

Type of animal:

....

Colour:

....

Personality:

....

Favourite food:

....

Now draw a picture!

Name:

....

Type of animal:

....

Colour:

....

Personality:

....

Favourite food:

....

Now draw a picture!

Moana the brave

Moana has never left her home on Motunui before, so she has to be very brave as she journeys across the sea. She never gives up, even when things seem impossible. Do you know anyone who is as brave as Moana?

Someone who I think is really brave is:

....

I think they're brave because:

....

....

....

Moana uses her warrior face to scare off monsters. Even when you're frightened on the inside, sometimes you need to look brave on the outside – and just keep trying!

Think of a time when you were really brave and write all about it here. Then, if you ever feel scared, you can look back here and remember how brave you really are!

A time when I was really brave was:

....

....

....

....

....

....

....

....

....

....

....

....

Monster mayhem

Moana meets lots of strange and frightening creatures on her journey – like the Kakamora, scary little bandits in coconut armour, and Te Kā, the fiery lava monster! Try designing your own monsters below. They can be scary or silly, huge or tiny – whatever you want!

This monster is:
- ◯ Scary
- ◯ Friendly
- ◯ Silly
- ◯ Grumpy
- ◯ Shy
- ◯ Playful

Where does it live?

....

What does it eat?

....

Is it big or small?

....

Draw your monster here:

Give your monster a name: ....

This monster is:

- ⚪ Scary
- ⚪ Friendly
- ⚪ Silly
- ⚪ Grumpy
- ⚪ Shy
- ⚪ Playful

Where does it live?

....

What does it eat?

....

Is it big or small?

....

Draw your monster here:

Give your monster a name:

....

This monster is:

- ⚪ Scary
- ⚪ Friendly
- ⚪ Silly
- ⚪ Grumpy
- ⚪ Shy
- ⚪ Playful

Where does it live?

....

What does it eat?

....

Is it big or small?

....

Draw your monster here:

Give your monster a name:

....